THE BOXCAR CHILDREN

Withdrawn Print

Time to Read™

Time to Read™ is an early reader program designed to guide children to literacy success regardless of age or grade level. The program's three levels correspond to stages of reading readiness, making book selection straightforward, and assuring that when it's time for a child to read, the right book is waiting.

— Level — 1

Beginning to Read

- Large, simple type
- Basic vocabulary
- Word repetition
- Strong illustration support

— Level — 2

Reading with Help

- Short sentences
- Engaging stories
- Simple dialogue
- Illustration support

— Level — 3

Reading Independently

- Longer sentences
- Harder words
- Short paragraphs
- Increased story complexity

Library of Congress Cataloging-in-Publication data is on file with the publisher.

Copyright © 2018 by Albert Whitman & Company
Hardcover edition first published in the United States of America
in 2018 by Albert Whitman & Company
Paperback edition first published in the United States of America
in 2019 by Albert Whitman & Company
ISBN 978-0-8075-0835-0

Printed in China
10 9 8 7 6 5 4 3 2 1 WKT 22 21 20 19 18

Cover and interior art by Shane Clester

Visit the Boxcar Children online at www.boxcarchildren.com.
For more information about Albert Whitman & Company,
visit our website at www.albertwhitman.com.

100 Years of Albert Whitman & Company
Celebrate with us in 2019!

THE BOXCAR CHILDREN®

THE BOXCAR CHILDREN

Based on the book by
Gertrude Chandler Warner

Albert Whitman & Company
Chicago, Illinois

One night four children stood outside of a bakery.

The children were hungry and needed a place to sleep.

They did not have a home.

Henry and Jessie Alden were the two oldest children.

They took care of their sister, Violet, and brother, Benny.

"Let's go in and buy some bread," said Henry.

Jessie nodded.

"Maybe they will let us spend the night," she said.

Inside, Henry paid for the bread.
Then Jessie asked the woman
if they could stay.
Jessie explained that they
were orphans.
Their parents had died.

"Can't you stay with
your grandparents?"
the woman asked.
"We have a grandfather,"
said Benny.
"But he doesn't like us."
The children had never
met their grandfather.
He had not visited, so they
thought he was mean.
The woman sighed.
She let them spend the night.

The children lay on
soft benches.
They were safe and warm
in the bakery.
Had the Aldens found
their new home?

Jessie heard voices in
the next room.
It was the woman and her husband.
"The older ones can stay and
work," the woman said.
"But the little one is too young."
The bakers were
going to send
Benny away!
Jessie woke
the others.
Quietly, they
left the bakery.

The children walked and walked.
When the sun came up,
they stopped.

Henry did not think they
should walk in daylight.
He was afraid their grandfather
might find them.
The children found haystacks
and made little nests.
Soon they were fast asleep.

It was night when
the children awoke.
Jessie cut some bread for supper.
Then they started to
walk again.

Before long, dark clouds
covered the moon.
It began to rain.
"Let's go into the forest,"
said Henry.
"The trees will help keep us dry."

The rain came down harder.
"We need to find shelter!"
said Violet.
Lightning flashed.
"I think I see something,"
 said Jessie. "Come on!"
The children ran.

It was an old boxcar!

Henry slid open the door.

He helped Violet inside.

Then Benny and Jessie

climbed in.

Outside, the wind howled.

The rain fell and fell.

But no water came in.

When the rain stopped,
the children stepped outside.
A stream flowed nearby.
"It's beautiful!" said Jessie.
"Let's live here!"
But Benny wasn't so sure.
"Won't a train come?" he asked.
Henry smiled.
"No trains go this way,
Benny. See?"
He showed Benny bushes
growing on the tracks.
This made Benny feel better.
The children agreed to make
the boxcar their new home.

In the afternoon, Henry
went to buy food.
Jessie, Violet, and Benny
explored.
"Blueberry bushes!" said Violet,
running ahead.
Then she heard a strange noise
and stopped.

It was coming from the bushes.
"I think it's a bear," said Benny.
But it was not a bear...
It was a dog!

"He seems nice," said Jessie.
"But I think he's hurt."
Jessie saw a thorn in the
dog's paw.
She pulled it out.
Slowly, the dog wagged its tail.

When Henry came back,
the dog barked.
"Can we keep him?" asked Violet.

"Well," said Henry, "he does
seem like a good watchdog!"
"That's what his name will be!"
said Benny. "Watch!"

Jessie set out supper.
It was the children's biggest
meal in days.

They even had enough for
their watchdog!

After supper, the children
went back to the boxcar.
"This side will be the
bedroom," Jessie said.
She and Henry made beds
out of pine needles.
It was a small start.
But the boxcar was starting
to feel like home.

In the morning, Henry walked
to town.

The children needed money,
and Henry was old enough
to work.

He met a man named
Doctor Moore, who paid him
to cut grass.

Doctor Moore saw that Henry
was a good worker.
But where had the boy
come from?

While Henry worked, Jessie,
Violet, and Benny explored.
"We're looking for treasure!"
said Jessie.
"Cans, bottles, dishes."
"Those things are treasure?"
asked Benny.
"They will be to us!" Jessie said.
Benny found a big
garbage dump.
He climbed to the top and
held up a pink cup.
It had a crack in it.
But Jessie was right.
It was treasure to him.

For the next few weeks, Henry
worked at Doctor Moore's.
He took care of the garden.
He cut the grass.
He cleaned the garage.

Jessie, Violet, and Benny
worked on the boxcar.
Soon they had dishes and
shelves and pots and pans.
Violet even sewed a tablecloth.
There was just one thing missing.

The children went down
to the stream.
Henry and Jessie pulled logs
into the water.
Violet and Benny stacked
up stones.
The water got deeper.
Soon they had made their own
swimming pool!
Their little house was
now complete.

The next day, Doctor Moore
needed more helpers.
Jessie, Violet, and Benny
all wanted to come along.
But Henry was worried.
"Grandfather will be looking
for a group of four," he said.
So the children went in twos.
First Henry and Benny walked
to Doctor Moore's.
Then Jessie and Violet
came with Watch.

At Doctor Moore's, the children
helped with the cherry harvest.
Henry, Jessie, and Violet picked
the cherries.
Benny helped carry the baskets.
They all ate their fill.

As the children worked, Doctor
Moore read the newspaper.
He saw that a man was looking
for four lost children.
Doctor Moore looked at his helpers.
Could they be the missing children?
He would soon find out.

Not long after the harvest,
Violet started to feel sick.
"She cannot stay in the boxcar,"
said Jessie.
"We need to get help."
Henry ran to Doctor Moore's.
Doctor Moore came right away.
He saw the boxcar.
"These *are* the children from
the newspaper," he thought.
"They are hiding from
their grandfather!"
Doctor Moore brought the
children to his house.

Slowly, Violet got better.
Then one day the doctor
had a visitor.
"Children, meet Mr. Henry,"
Doctor Moore said.
Benny laughed.
"Henry and Mr. Henry!"

The children liked having
Mr. Henry around.
He read to Violet.
He played games with
Benny and Watch.
He even gave Henry
a pocketknife.

Then Henry noticed
something.

Mr. Henry's pocketknife had
three letters on it: *JHA*.

He knew the *H* meant *Henry*.

But what did the *J* and the *A*
stand for?

Henry asked Doctor Moore,
"Does Mr. Henry have
another name?"
The doctor smiled.
"Yes, his full name is James
Henry Alden."
Henry could not believe it!
Alden was
the children's
last name
too!

Henry went to Mr. Henry.

"You are our grandfather!"
he said.

Mr. Henry nodded.

Then he explained.

"Doctor Moore told me you
were hiding from me.

We didn't want to scare you.

So we kept my name secret."

"We're sorry we hid from you,"
said Jessie.

"If we knew you, we would
not have run."

"Yeah!" said Benny.
"We thought our grandfather
was old!
And mean!
You are great!"
Everyone laughed.

When Violet was better,
Mr. Henry brought the children
to his house.
Benny's eyes got big.
"You live here?" he asked.

"It can be your house too,"
Mr. Henry said.
"If you want it to be."
The children agreed.
They all wanted to live with
their grandfather.
"I will miss our little house
though," said Jessie.
Their grandfather smiled.
He led them to the backyard,
where a surprise was waiting.
It was just the thing to make
their new house…

home.

5